fade into you

by

leanne fogarty

We all have a story

torn out of someone

else's book

fade into you | leanne fogarty

PROLOGUE

We all have a story torn out of someone else's book. This is a captivating story, poetic in nature, yet as complete as any relationship that's run its course.

Leanne Fogarty tells the story of two lovers who have seamlessly gone from the sensation of finding true love to the realization their time has come to an end.

Told from the perspective of a personified novel, we feel the depth and meaning behind the metaphor.

We ourselves are all a book to be read, told, explored. We too can find ourselves stuck in someone else's story from time to time.

This artfully crafted story calls for a reflection on how we can all do a little better with the stories we find ourselves in and with the relationships we wish to create.

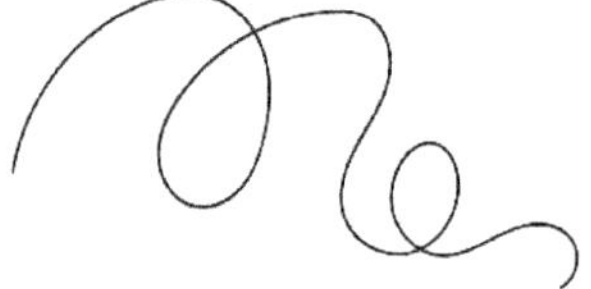

FADE INTO YOU

Two stories once came together as a book from beginning to end, with longing, loving, washed out daydreams.

An attempt at a life together. One person is day, the other is night. One person sees red, the other sees blue. One slips slowly into their morning routine, making sure to check off every box on their list, while the other rushes out the door.

One star-gazes, while the other longs for the sun to come up.

One prefers their coffee black and hot, while the other frequently forgets to drink their tea and allows it to cool before taking a sip. One's winter, one's summer. One's bright, sunny days, one's thunderstorms with dark clouds, and loud roars of thunder.

And yet, these differences faded into a brand-new set of poems, love letters, flowers, fading in coloured vases, 2 a.m. conversations, and timelines crashing, trying to make sense of how they even came together.

He was the background of a crowded theatre, and she was the spotlight on which all eyes fell

They somehow came together and slipped into each other, becoming the grey, meeting in the middle to tell the stories people usually skip over.

They knew their story wasn't the brightest nor the darkest, it was the only shade each of them could have dissolved into.

They made it make sense, like squared winged birds, acid teardrops, and a year with only 100 days.

But now, as one season rolls into the next, all the things that once made sense just sit there, like the almost perfect apple that was left with little attention, starting to mold and lose its colour, starting to shift its shape.

It can still look pretty on the outside, but biting into it could turn your stomach raw.

And swallowing just a very small piece will bring you back to the bitter reality of how something so beautiful starts to decompose.

A little bit of sweetness, a little bit of poison.

And the grey of them slid back into just white and just black and the mixing of the two together now feels like it never belonged.

One longs for the night so that they can dream, the other longs for the day so that they can go.

And all the stories that were written together can now be bought separately on the corner for less than a dollar, spread out among other books and magazine stands – that random people will never full heartedly care for or make sense of.

The memories will fade away with the letters on the page. And people will feel, laugh, love, and cry with the sentences that hit between their eyes, chapters that will never really be felt again.

A book that once came together, now split in two - for one, it's an ending, for the other it's a beginning - off to find another lonely story to slip into. Finding new ways to complete it from beginning to end, with torn out pages and fuzzy lines in between, different stories to remember, forget, and create, and the front and back a little ruffled.

This time, this story won't be sold. Instead, it will be kept on a corner shelf, collecting dust, to be used during heated conversations and nights that go on for far too long.

Whipping out old situations, words that were spilled out in moments of underestimated, overwhelmed hearts and foggy movements.

Things that don't even make sense because they come from other stories that were written with different people whose faces had faded out years before. It won't need to be thrown away. This one can be kept around to re-read, re-feel, re-learn, to remember what was, now is, and can be.

But it can't be a favourite book - not this one, not for you. It's not the type of book where you breathe in and then out with relief - that you figured out the characters' wrongdoings and true blessings. It's not the type of book where when you close it and let yourself sit there for a few moments to take in, just to release it, and then fall asleep.

You won't be able to let it go so easily because these are the stories that have been tagging along behind you, all while you've been gaining years.

These are the stories that have kept you up at night, trying to spin the alphabet around while you try to make sense of what happened.

Words from these pages are words that you have let carry on from one person to the next, one place to the other, all while acting like you've closed the book for good, giving the illusion that you're ready to start over.

You wanted people to read you, so that they could understand even the smallest piece of you, the tucked away and hidden parts.

But they acted like you were just some other book - left open on some random shelf, that they didn't have time for.

So now you sit alone thinking of what to write next, how to express stories from previous years.

Don't be so surprised when you use some of the same words, from some of your old stories, for when you create a story from the wounds you think will be just like the rest.

But this time, you will try to put a different spin on it, to make it feel far away from what you've written before. You will realize you are worth every word cluttered onto the page, every unfinished sentence you're not able to end, every piece that has never come together.

Every person that's read you and misunderstood, has come strolling along from their own story they wrote, their own pages that have been torn out.

Just know, you will fade into grey, with someone new, who already knows the exact same words as you, and who has the same chapters faded out.

And you'll come together and slip into each other, becoming the shade that meets in the middle.

And it will all make sense, like watered plants, tea at 3, and a year that has 365 days.

The Coldest Moment

It smells of morning dew and secret.
Those secrets you held as I walked
out the door. You didn't even try to
stop me. I wanted to stop, to see,
to breathe, in the coldest moment
of the season.

The   windows   are   frosted   with
heaviness from last nights screams,
words not meant to be said.

Tire marks in snowy driveways.
I'm so cold I didn't pack for this

weather. Who knows where I'll end up.
If it's not by your side, I think I'd
rather just freeze.

I don't turn around.
I hear the door close.
I know where you stand as I stand
alone.

My cheeks turn red, my eyes a
different shade of blue. Out here
slipping and sliding in this
driveway, trying to make it all stop.

The air feels different. The houses
all look the same. The neighbours are

watching like every other day. The difference this time is that you're keeping that door closed, and I am out here alone crying.

THE BEGINNING

An attempt at a life together

one person is day,
          the other is night.

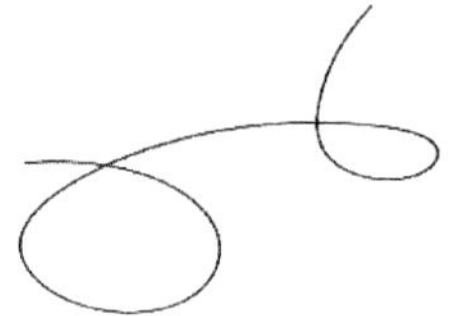

One person sees red, the other sees blue. One slips slowly into their morning routine, making sure to check off every box on their list, while the other rushes out the door.

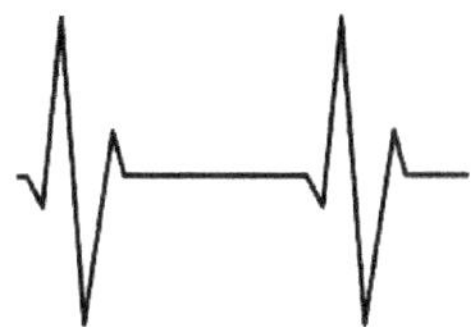

One star-gazes, while the other longs
for the sun to come up.

One prefers their coffee black and hot, while the other frequently forgets to drink their tea and allows it to cool before taking a sip.

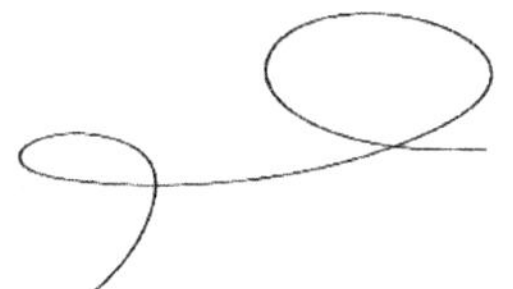

One's winter, one's summer.

One's bright, sunny days, one's thunderstorms with dark clouds, and loud roars of thunder.

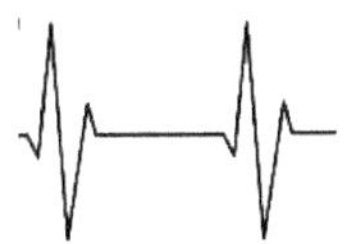

And yet, these differences faded into a brand-new set of poems, love letters, flowers, fading in coloured vases, 2 a.m. conversations, and timelines crashing, trying to make sense of how they even came together.

He was the background of a crowded
theatre, and she was the spotlight
on which all eyes fell

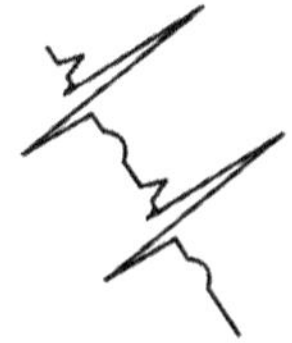

They somehow came together and
slipped into each other, becoming the
grey, meeting in the middle to tell
the stories people usually skip over

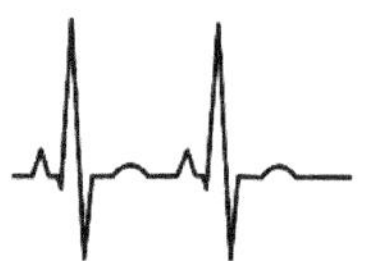

They knew their story wasn't the brightest nor the darkest, it was the only shade each of them could have dissolved into.

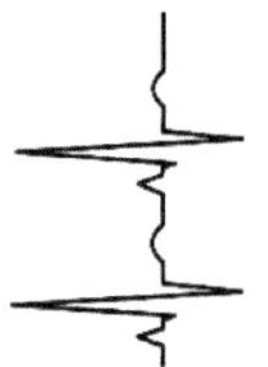

They made it make sense, like squared winged birds, acid teardrops, and a year with only 100 days.

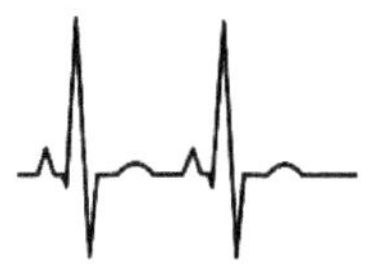

THE MIDDLE

But now, as one season rolls into the next, all the things that once made sense just sit there, like the almost perfect apple that was left with little attention, starting to mold and lose its colour, starting to shift its shape.

It can still look pretty on the outside, but biting into it could turn your stomach raw.

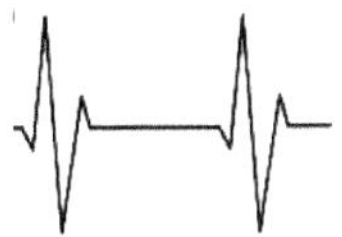

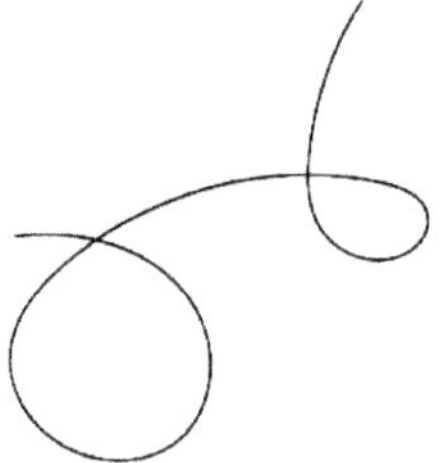

And swallowing just a very small

piece will bring you back to the
bitter reality of how something so
beautiful starts to decompose.

A little bit of sweetness, a little bit of poison.

And the grey of them slid back into just white and just black and the mixing of the two together now feels like it never belonged.

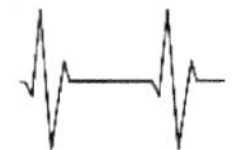

One longs for the night so that they can dream, the other longs for the day so that they can go.

And all the stories that were written
together can now be bought separately
on the corner for less than a dollar,

spread out among other books and magazine stands, that random people will never full heartedly care for or make sense of.

and people will feel, laugh, love, and cry with the sentences that hit between their eyes, chapters that will never really be felt again.

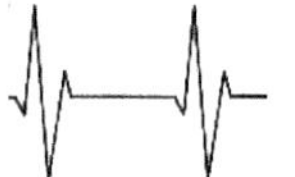

And a book that once came together, now split in two. For one, it's an ending, for the other, it's a beginning, off to find another lonely story to slip into

Finding new ways to complete it from beginning to end, with torn out pages.

and fuzzy lines in between, different
stories to remember, forget, and
create, and the front and back a
little ruffled.

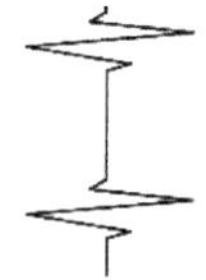

THE ENDING

This time, this story won't be sold.

Instead, it will be kept on a corner shelf, collecting dust, to be used during heated conversations and nights that go on for far too long.

Whipping out old situations, words that were spilled out in moments of underestimated, overwhelmed hearts and foggy moments.

Things that don't even make sense because they come from other stories that were written with different people whose faces had faded out years before.

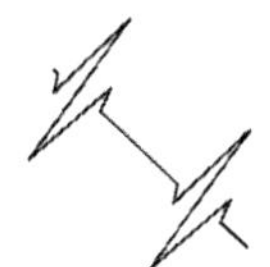

But it won't need to be thrown away. This one can be kept around to re-read, re-feel, re-learn, to remember what was, now is, and can be.

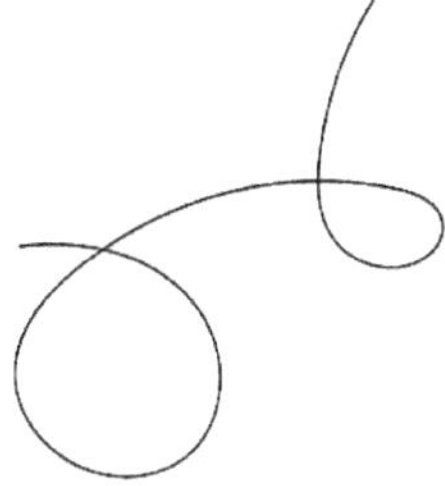

But it can't be a favourite book -
not this one, not for you.

It's not the type of book where you
breathe in and then out with relief

that you figured out the characters'
wrongdoings and true blessings.

It's not the type of book where when
you close it and let yourself sit
there for a few moments to take in,

just to release it, and then fall
asleep.

You won't be able to let it go so easily because these are the stories that have been tagging along behind you, all while you've been gaining years.

These are the stories that have kept
you up at night, trying to spin the
alphabet around while you try to make
sense of what happened.

Words from these pages are words that you have let carry on from one person to the next, one place to the other, all while acting like you've closed the book for good, giving the illusion that you're ready to start over.

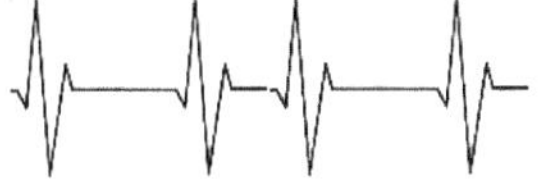

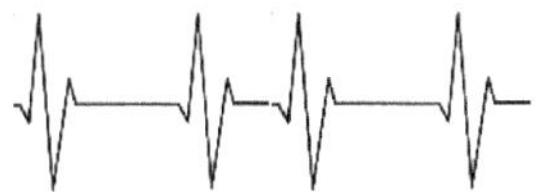

You wanted people to read you, so that they could understand even the smallest piece of you, the tucked away and hidden parts of you.

But they acted like you were just some other book - left open on some random shelf, that they didn't have time for.

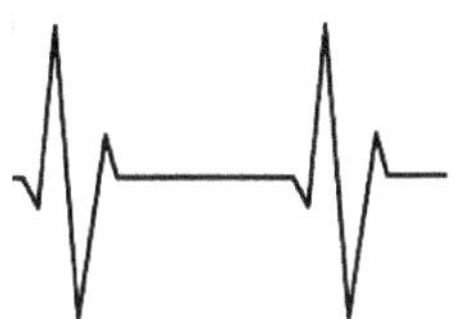

So now you sit alone thinking of what
to write next, how to express stories
from previous years.

Don't be so surprised when you use
some of the same words, from some of
your old stories, for when you create
a story from the wounds you think
will be just like the rest.

But this time, you try to put a
different spin on it, to make it feel
far away from what you've written
about before

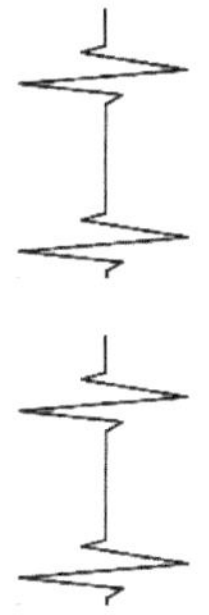

You will realize you are worth every word cluttered onto the page, every unfinished sentence you're not able to end, every piece that has never come together

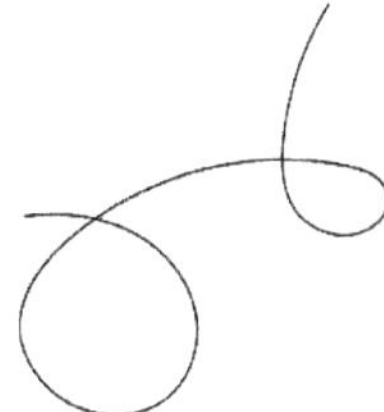

And that every person that's read you and misunderstood, that has come strolling along from their own story they wrote, their own pages that have been torn out

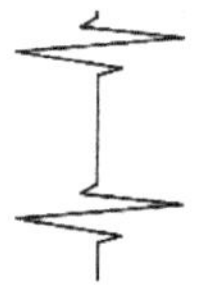

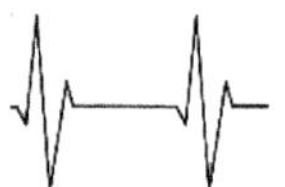

You'll fade to grey, with someone new, who already knows the exact same words as you, and who has the same chapters faded out

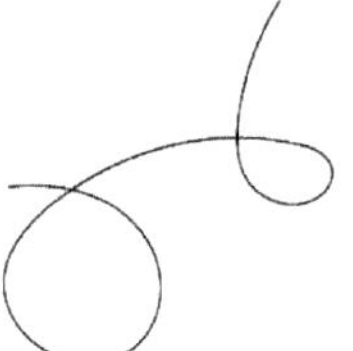

And you'll come together and slip
into each other

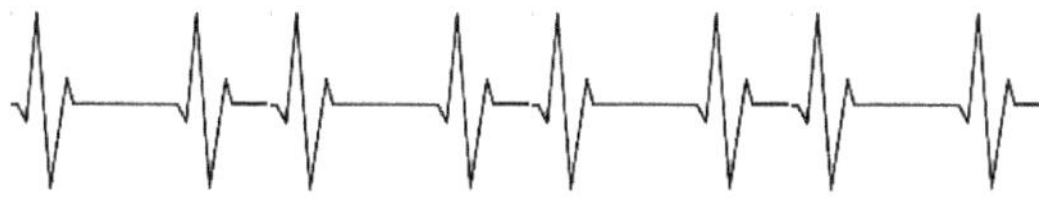

And it will all make sense: like
watered plants, tea at 3, and a year
that has 365 days.

This section is for you to

write your own story...

Use the writing prompts

to guide you

Writing Prompt:

If you could tell any story,

what would it be?

Writing Prompt:

Have you ever fallen in love?

Writing Prompt:

Tell me a secret

Writing Prompt:

What's your favorite

food and why?

Writing Prompt:

When was the last

time you wrote a

story?

Writing Prompt:

Are you the main character

of your life?

Writing Prompt:

Who else do you see

in your story?

Writing Prompt:

Where do you see yourself

ten years from now?

Writing Prompt:

Are you the hero or the

villain in your story?